D0528796

CINDEREL
THE REAL STORY

The Criminal Investigation
of Cinderella Nottapenny

Evidence gathered by D.I. Whiskers and
P.C. Scratch, Private Investigators

Case file presented by
Jan Burchett and Sara Vogler
Artist's impressions by Omar Aranda

Turn to page 35 for
The Continued Crimes of
Cinderella Nottapenny

Published by Pearson Education Limited, Edinburgh Gate, Harlow, Essex, CM20 2JE
Registered company number: 872828

www.pearsonschools.co.uk

Text © Jan Burchett and Sara Vogler 2011

Designed by Bigtop
Original illustrations © Pearson Education 2011
Illustrated by Omar Aranda
Printed and bound at Malaysia (CTP-PJB)

The rights of the authors' names to be identified as authors of this work have been asserted by
them in accordance with the Copyright, Designs and Patents Act 1988.

First published 2011

15
10 9 8 7 6 5

British Library Cataloguing in Publication Data
A catalogue record for this book is available from the British Library

ISBN 978 1 408 27410 1

Copyright notice
All rights reserved. No part of this publication may be reproduced in any form or by any means
(including photocopying or storing it in any medium by electronic means and whether or not
transiently or incidentally to some other use of this publication) without the written permission
of the copyright owner, except in accordance with the provisions of the Copyright, Designs and
Patents Act 1988 or under the terms of a licence issued by the Copyright Licensing Agency,
Saffron House, 6–10 Kirby Street, London EC1N 8TS (www.cla.co.uk). Applications for the
copyright owner's written permission should be addressed to the publisher.

Acknowledgements
We would like to thank the children and teachers of Bangor Primary School, Bangor; Bishop
Henderson C of E Primary School, Radstock, Somerset; Brookside Community Primary School,
Street, Somerset; Cheddington Combined School, Buckinghamshire; Cofton Primary School,
Birmingham; Dair House Independent School, Buckinghamshire; Newbold Riverside School,
Rugby and Clifton Hampden C of E Primary School, Oxfordshire for their invaluable help in
the development and trialling of the Bug Club resources.

Every effort has been made to contact copyright holders of material reproduced in this book.
Any omissions will be rectified in subsequent printings if notice is given to the publishers.

From: roland.nottapenny@onceuponatime.com
Sent: 24 September 10:31
To: cedric.nottapenny@far.far.away.land.com
Subject: Urgent help needed!

Dear Cedric,

I need some advice from you – after all, isn't that what big brothers are for? I'm at my wits' end.
I need to get my three girls married. My dear stepdaughters, Bethany and Megan, are good, kind girls, but they're so ugly they'd crack a mirror. Look at the awful photo at the end of this email! I took it last week. Poor girls. If only men would just take the trouble to get to know them, they'd soon see how lovely they are.

On the other hand, there's my daughter Cinderella – there's no doubt that she's beautiful, and she has men falling over each other to go on a date with her – but then they find out how awful she is. Last week she threw her drink over one lovely young gentleman, just because, *she* said, his teeth weren't

→

straight! Well, they looked perfectly straight to me. Last month, she stomped on another man's foot with her high heels when she discovered he didn't live in a castle! At home, she calls me Old Meanie, throws food at the cat and sits with her feet up all day while her poor stepsisters do the scrubbing and sweeping.

Cinders also insists on wearing rags just to show me up. She pretends I won't buy her anything pretty to wear, even though I spend all of my hard-earned money on the latest fashions for her.

This situation is driving me mad – I need your help. Please reply as soon as you can.

Roland

↰ Reply   → Forward

From: cedric.nottapenny@far.far.away.land.com
Sent: 24 September 13:08
To: roland.nottapenny@onceuponatime.com
Subject: Answer to your problem

Dear Roland,

Great to hear from you, old chap. I may just have the answer!

Prince Charming is hosting a ball for all the young women in the kingdom so that he can choose a wife. Make sure that your three go. Maybe Bethany and Megan could wear masks?

Imagine being father to a princess!

Cedric

↩ Reply   → Forward

From: roland.nottapenny@onceuponatime.com
Sent: 24 September 16:42
To: cedric.nottapenny@far.far.away.land.com
Subject: Thanks, brother!

My dear brother Cedric,

That sounds perfect! Great idea – I'll send Beth and Megan in masks so that the boys can't see their faces. Then perhaps they will have a chance to get to know how sweet they both are.

I'll give Cinders a big gobstopper to take with her. That should keep her quiet!

Roland

↩ Reply → Forward

6

Invitation

To: Bethany, Megan and Cinderella

Please come to: my ball
At: my palace
Time: 8pm
Date: Saturday 30th September

From: Prince Charming

R.S.V.P. to The Palace, King's Road, Onceuponatime Town.

p.s. Ballgowns must be worn
p.p.s. ... but only by the ladies.

Fairytale Friends

The magical friendship site for fairytale folk

Remember: Stay away from the Big Bad Wolf. Only talk to characters you know and trust.

 UglySis1: Cool! We've had an invitation to the prince's ball! Can't wait. It would be awesome to marry Prince Charming but I bet he'll choose Cinderella. She's the beautiful one.

 Miss_RidingHood: She wasn't very nice at school though. She said my grandma had a hairy face.

 Rapunzel: She was mean! Once she glued my plaits to the radiator.

 Goldilox: She used to eat all the porridge at school breakfast. There was none left for me!

Friends online now

✓	Miss_RidingHood
✓	Rapunzel
✓	Goldilox
✓	ClumsyHumpty
✓	SnoWhite

 ClumsyHumpty: She pushed me off my wall – three times! The king's men had to keep putting me back together again.

 SnoWhite: She presented me with a red apple.

 UglySis1: Well that was nice of her. See – she's not all bad.

 SnoWhite: It was full of poison! I was in hospital for 3 weeks. Even Happy was sad.

Shopping list

Loaf of bread

Three tomatoes

Half a tin of baked beans

Porridge

A NEW DRESS
(Take note, Dad. It had better be silk and
covered with jewels, and I need new shoes
to go with it too. Glass slippers would
be perfect. If you don't buy them now,
I'll scream the house down.
I mean it!
Cinderella)

Dear Cinders,

I'm going to slip this note under your door as you won't let anyone in while you're screaming the house down. Daddy tried to explain to you that after paying for your magazines, perfumes and trumpet lessons, he doesn't have any money left to buy you a gown. But don't worry — I have a nearly new dress that I can alter to fit you. It'll look lovely on you. Bethany says you can wear her best necklace. You will look beautiful.

Cinderella, you <u>will</u> go to the ball!

Love Megan xx

From: Cinderella
25 September   13:09

To Megan Monkeyface. Keep your smelly old dress. I'm not going out in your ugly second-hand things. And tell Bethany Big Nose her necklace looks like a dog's collar!

Reply

Things going badly?
Wishes never come true?
I can help you!

email: f.godmother@happy.ever.after.com

All wishes are subject to a fee on a pay-per-wish basis. No responsibility is taken for clients who are accidentally turned into frogs or any other pond life.

From: pretty_cinders@onceuponatime.com
Sent: 26 September 11:02
To: f.godmother@happy.ever.after.com
Subject: Me

Dear Fairy Godmother,

I need your help. I want to marry the prince.

Reply immediately.

Cinderella Nottapenny
(the future Princess Charming)

↰ Reply → Forward

From: f.godmother@happy.ever.after.com
Sent: 26 September 11:05
To: pretty_cinders@onceuponatime.com
Subject: You

Attachment: ProjectPrincess.doc

Dear Cinderella,

Thank you for your email about marrying the prince. Nothing could be simpler! Everything you want will be yours with one* wave of my magic wand.

The ball is the perfect place to get yourself that royal bridegroom. To catch the prince's eye, you've got to stick out from the crowd, so we need a plan. Please see the attached document for details.

Yours sincerely,
Fairy Godmother

* One wave included in fee. All extra waves are £5 each. Special offer this month – buy nine get one free.

Reply   Forward

Project Princess ★ ★ ★ ★

The Plan

You make a late and spectacular entrance at the ball to get you noticed, so stay behind when your stepsisters go. Tell them that you refuse to be seen in public without the dress of your dreams.

I'll magic you up a fabulous dress and some dainty glass slippers for your dainty little feet. Magic dresses and dainty glass slippers always charm princes.

I will sort out your transport when I get to you on Saturday. I have some ideas up my sleeve.

p.s. All spells last until midnight. It's double fees after that.

From: fairy.g.assistant@happy.ever.after.com
Sent: 28 September 10:33
To: pretty_cinders@onceuponatime.com
Subject: Further details

Dear Miss Nottapenny,

Your fairy godmother will be with you at 8pm sharp on Saturday 30th September. Be in your kitchen ready for her arrival. Once you are ready, you will go to Mary Mary's garden to locate a pumpkin.

Hoping you live happily ever after,

Polly

(Assistant to Fairy Godmother)

Item 7: Radio conversation between D.I. Whiskers, who was relaxing at his home in Nottapenny Cottage, and P.C. Scratch, who was out hunting for cheesecake

Whiskers: Hello, Scratch? Don't come back to Nottapenny Cottage. A fairy godmother has just appeared in the kitchen!

Scratch: Oh no! Fairy godmothers are always bad news. Remember when Uncle Scrabblepaws got turned into a flying carpet for Aladdin? He still feels faint at the sight of a vacuum cleaner! Who called this fairy godmother? I hope she's here for Megan or Bethany. They're such lovely girls – it's a pleasure to live under their floorboards.

Whiskers: No, she's come for Cinderella.

Scratch: Oh no! That horrible girl! Everyone thinks she's so lovely until they get to know her. She tried to hit me with a cucumber the other day. She doesn't deserve a fairy godmother!

Whiskers: Well, she's got one. The fairy godmother is saying she's come to help Cinderella look all glamorous for the prince's ball. You know those rags she's been wearing to upset her dad and show everyone how poor she is? Well, the fairy godmother has waved her wand and changed them into a really elegant ball gown! It's covered in sparkly jewels!

Scratch: A posh gown won't make her any nicer to be around.

Whiskers: Now she's turned Cinderella's old trainers into a pair of dainty glass slippers! Magic!

Scratch:	I hope those slippers give her blisters!
Whiskers:	Too right. Uh oh! The fairy godmother has caught Cousin Nibbler. She's holding her up by the tail. What's she doing? Argh, she's turned her into a coach driver!
Scratch:	Poor Nibbler. Still, I suppose it's better than being a flying carpet. Can't you do anything to save her?
Whiskers:	I'll bite that fairy godmother on the ankle.
Scratch:	Good plan!
Whiskers:	Uh oh. She's chasing me! Magic dust in my eyes! AHHHH ...
Scratch:	Whiskers? Whiskers? Are you all right?
Whiskers:	Neigh!

From: Fairy Godmother
30 September   20:10

Polly – here's a quick update. Arrived safely at client's house. Almost everything is ready. Just need to find pumpkin to turn into a carriage. Will get client to help me. Will bewitch myself so no one sees me. Can't bewitch client though or she'd still be invisible for the ball. Hope no one sees her!

ONCEUPONATIME TOWN
○ POLICE STATION ○

Crime Report

Date and time: 30 September 8:22pm
Crime reported by: Mary Mary
Phone call taken by: Sergeant Bigbear

Sergeant: Onceuponatime Town police station. Sergeant Bigbear speaking. How can I help?

Mary Mary: It's Mary Mary here.

Sergeant: Hello there, Mary Mary. How does your garden grow?

Mary Mary: Not very well! I want to report a theft.

Sergeant: What's been stolen?

Mary Mary: A pumpkin – and not just any old pumpkin. It was the biggest, roundest, shiniest pumpkin from my prize vegetable patch.

Sergeant: That's dreadful, Mary Mary. Did you see who took this perfect pumpkin?

Mary Mary: Yes, I think it was that miserable girl next door who dresses in rags – except that tonight she was wearing a jewel-encrusted ball gown and glass slippers and she was holding *my* pumpkin! Then all of a sudden, from nowhere, there was a bang and a shower of sparkles and the pumpkin disappeared. Instead there was this huge horse-drawn coach standing right in the middle of my vegetable patch. That horrible girl got in and the carriage charged off towards the palace, trampling my rhubarb on its way.

Sergeant: Your prize rhubarb, Mary Mary? The prize rhubarb you use for your prize-winning rhubarb crumble?

Mary Mary: The very same. All completely ruined. There'll be no rhubarb crumble this year.

Sergeant: Now that *is* a crime!

From: Fairy Godmother
30 September   20:18

Polly, put the kettle on. I'll be home in a flash. Cinderella is on her way to the palace and if she's not engaged to the prince by midnight, I'll eat my wand. Put the telly on too – I want to watch the ball on 'I'm a Prince: Get Me a Bride!'

Hansel: Welcome to *I'm a Prince: Get Me a Bride!* I'm Hansel and this is the lovely Gretel.

Gretel: Thanks Hansel. The Royal Ball is off to a magical start. Look at these ladies arriving in their fabulous designer dresses.

Hansel: Ooh – that girl has an enormous nose!

Gretel: And that one looks like a monkey!

25

Hansel: Who's this arriving?

Gretel: I don't know ... but, my goodness,
           isn't she beautiful!

Hansel: She's making straight for the prince.
           He looks totally bewitched!

Gretel: Could we soon be hearing the sound
           of wedding bells?

POLICE RAID AT PALACE BALL

Attacker gets her just desserts

by crime reporter Margery Daw

THERE WAS PANIC at the palace last night as an unknown guest ran amok during Prince Charming's ball. The beautiful stranger began the night in fine style, making a dramatic entrance from an elegant coach. Sweeping up the red carpet, she brought the dancing to a complete halt with her sudden entrance.

Prince Charming was clearly bowled over by the sight of the gorgeous lady in her stunning jewel-encrusted silk gown and dainty glass slippers, although so far nobody has been able to identify her.

"His mother had to tell him to stop

gawping like a goldfish," said one of the palace servants, who witnessed the event. "He wouldn't dance with any girl but her ... until the police arrived, that is."

Party guests described a sudden commotion as a burly police sergeant marched across the floor and made straight for the prince's mysterious dance partner.

"He tried to arrest her for criminal damage to a prize rhubarb patch and the theft of a pumpkin!" said the Sugar Plum Fairy, a guest at the ball. Things then took a turn for the worse as the girl took the prince hostage,

Witnesses heard the attacker say: "Keep away or I'll bash him with this baguette!"

threatening to hit him with a baguette if the police sergeant got any closer.

Thankfully, a quick-thinking guest saved the day by flinging a nearby trifle over the attacker's head, stopping her in her tracks. Unfortunately, the attacker managed to escape during the commotion that followed. She left behind a dainty glass slipper. Police are launching a search to find the owner of this glass slipper.

Stunned prince falls for his mystery masked rescuer as crowd chants "Hurrah! Our prince is saved!"

Fairytale Friends

The magical friendship site for fairytale folk

**Remember: Stay away from the Big Bad Wolf.
Only talk to characters you know and trust.**

UglySis2: Have you seen all my pics of the ball?

Miss_RidingHood: Love the one of Beth with the trifle bowl. Legend! LOL.

Rapunzel: We just had Sergeant Bigbear round here. He's making house-to-house enquiries. He's trying to find the mad woman who attacked the prince.

Goldilox: That's right. He came here too. We all have to try on the glass slipper she left behind to see if it fits. It was still full of custard when he came round to my house! I didn't eat it though – it was too cold. :-(

Friends online now

- ✓ Miss_RidingHood
- ✓ Rapunzel
- ✓ Goldilox
- ✓ UglySis2
- ✓ SnoWhite

SnoWhite: He came here but my feet are too big, thank goodness. I wonder whose it is?

UglySis2: Sergeant Bigbear has just been here. The slipper is Cinderella's! It fitted perfectly! She tried to escape up the chimney but he grabbed her by the ankles and pulled her down. She was dragged away, covered in soot! :-S

Fairytale Friends

UglySis1: Poor Cinders. I had no idea it was her when I splatted her with the trifle! She looked so different, all dressed up. Didn't even know she was there – she said she wasn't going if she couldn't get the dress she wanted!

UglySis2: We should've been suspicious when we got home and saw the trail of cream leading to her room.

SnoWhite: Look on the bright side, girls. At least your chimney's been cleaned.

Goldilox: And poor Cinders must be feeling a TRIFLE upset today! Geddit? LOL!

PRINCE CHARMING WEDS

Ding dong bell, Cinders in a cell

by royal reporter Tommy Stout

The sound of wedding bells rang out all over Onceuponatime Town yesterday to celebrate the marriage of the very charming Prince Charming to Bethany Nottapenny.

The happy couple met at the palace ball last week – and what a meeting! Bethany saved his royal life with a dessert when a vicious mystery guest held a baguette to his throat. Incredibly, following a police hunt for the owner of the glass slipper that was left behind, the attacker was identified as Cinderella Nottapenny, stepsister of the royal bride! Cinders, as she is known, is now locked up in prison following a short trial.

All the townsfolk gathered to watch the royal wedding. The bride wore a heavy veil and her bridesmaid, Megan, wore an elegant mask.

Friends and family of the couple say that the prince and his courageous princess are going to live happily ever after.

Added note: We apologise for the quality of the photo as our official photographer, Mr Dumpty, had a little accident with a wall. Again.

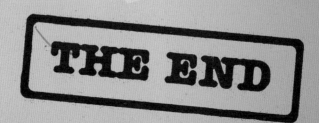

THE END

CINDERELLA:
THE REAL STORY

The Continued Crimes
of Cinderella Nottapenny

New evidence prepared by D.I. Whiskers and
P.C. Scratch, Private Investigators

Case file presented by
Jan Burchett and Sara Vogler
Artist's impressions by Omar Aranda

CINDERELLA: WHERE DID IT ALL GO WRONG?

What made this beautiful girl from a loving family turn to crime?

CINDERELLA NOTTAPENNY HAD it all – two kind stepsisters and a doting father who gave her everything he could. Yet still she wanted more.

When Prince Charming stepped up his search for a wife by holding a royal ball, Cinderella was determined to get her hands on the prince and his money. On the night of the ball, she stole a pumpkin and went joyriding over her neighbour's vegetable patch before heading for the palace. When police caught up with her, Cinderella, who was unrecognisably glamorous in a jewel-encrusted gown, threatened His Royal Highness with a baguette that she'd swiped from the banquet table.

Fortunately, the prince was saved by the quick thinking of Cinderella's brave stepsister, Bethany, who threw a trifle over Cinderella's head. The money-seeker's evil plans were thwarted and she was arrested on the spot.

In a romantic twist, the prince was so delighted to be rescued that he fell in love with his courageous rescuer and the pair were soon engaged. On the very day that wedding bells rang out for the royal couple, Cinderella was summoned to a short trial and was sent to Onceuponatime Town Prison for Storybook Villains, where she will serve her three-year sentence.

Cinderella's jailer, Jack the Giant Killer, told us, "We are very hopeful that Cinderella will soon be sorry for what she has done. She has a program of rehabilitation activities lined up, such as basket weaving and cookery classes, to help her become a model citizen."

Monday 9th October
8am
Time in jail so far: 3 days, 15 hours, 37 minutes and 4 seconds.

My jailer says I should keep a diary of all my thoughts and then I'll come to realise what a silly girl I have been. The only silly thing I've done is not ducking when that stupid Bethany Big Nose brained me with the trifle. I should be Mrs Prince Charming, not her, and I should be living at the palace covered in jewels. I'd be relishing banquets and cream cakes and chocolate every day – not suffering this disgusting prison slop! I'm not giving up.

Here's the plan:

1. Find someone unsavoury to get rid of Bethany Big Nose.
2. Make sure no one suspects I'm behind it.
3. Get out of here somehow.
4. Marry the prince.
5. Be a rich princess. Heh heh heh heh!

Off now to do basket weaving with Miss Muffet's spider. Apparently it will make me a model citizen. Pah! As IF!

Fairy Godmother Services
Secret Location

Dear Cinderella,

I'm sorry to hear that you did not live happily ever after, despite my wonderful spells. However, with my help you will not be in prison for long. Another wave or two of my magic wand* and you'll be sure to get your prince.

Warning: Do not attempt to eat the pie that this note is hidden in. I may be a great fairy godmother but I'm not much of a cook. Poor Hansel broke his teeth on the gingerbread I made him last week.

Magically ever after,

Your Fairy Godmother

*£10 a wave – sorry. Prices have gone up since I sent you to the ball.

To Fairy Godmother,

You are NOT a great fairy godmother. If you were, it would be ME married to the prince now instead of my ugly stepsister. So you can keep your stupid magic. I'm going to sort things out for myself. I'll find someone else to help me. It can't be that difficult.

Cinderella

Monday 9th October

11am

Time in jail: No time to count at the moment

Need to find someone to help me with my plan. They mustn't be averse to a spot of crime ... so a fellow prisoner would be ideal. So, who can I try?

Red Riding Hood's Wolf? Only eats grandmas.

Snow White's evil stepmother? Won't get past the mirror in the hall.

Giant from the top of the beanstalk? Might get stuck in the door.

Big Bad Wolf?? Hmm ...

- Doesn't like goody-goodies
- Gets released from prison tonight
- Will do anything for a good meal
- Has been practising his huffing and puffing since his problem with that house made of bricks

... perfect!

Plan: Tell Big Bad Wolf to blow the palace down with Bethany in it.
Result: Squashed stepsister. I marry the prince and become a princess. Success!
Next action: Speak to Big Bad Wolf. Got cookery class with him this afternoon – will sneak him a secret message then.

Item 4: What happened next
(artist's impressions)

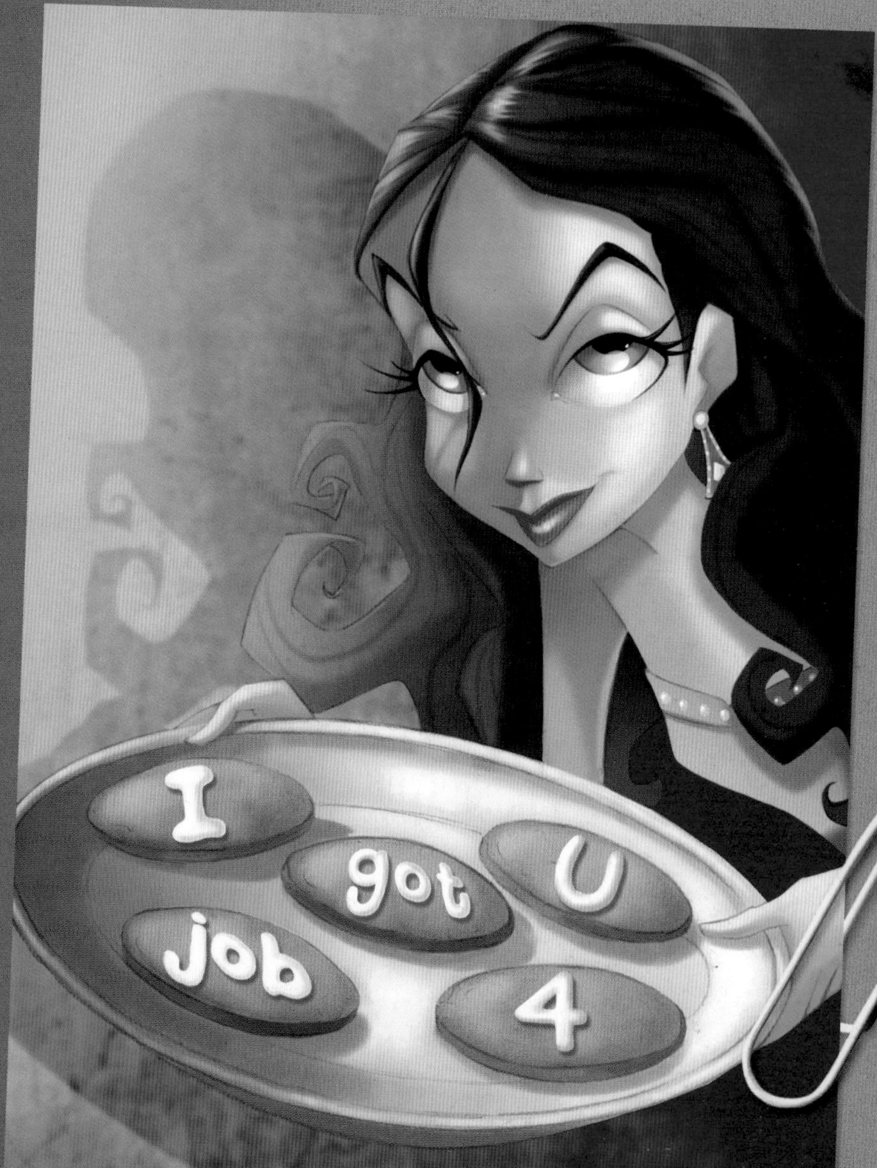

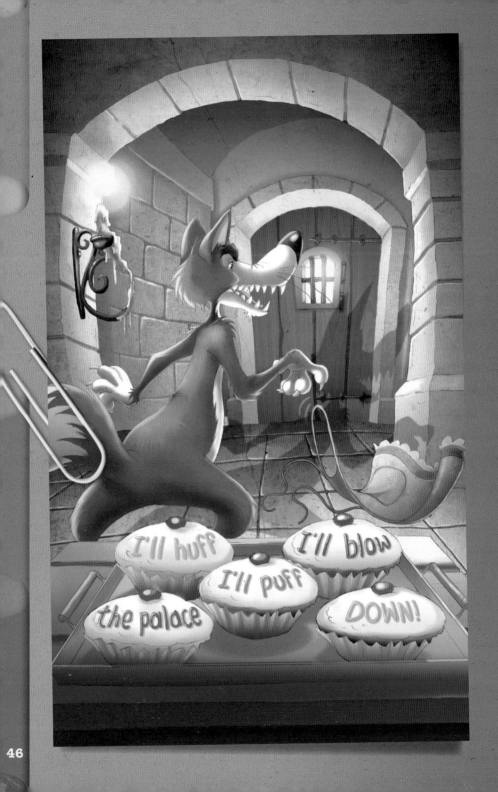

"You're listening to Onceuponatime Town Hospital Radio. This next message is for the Big Bad Wolf on Ward 5. The dedication comes from our lovely Princess Bethany. She found Mr Wolf outside the palace, flat on his back and gasping for breath. Princess Bethany is not sure what he was doing there, but she says, 'Get well soon, Wolfy.'

And now a song for royal photographer Humpty Dumpty, who's back in his usual bed following yet another accident with a wall ..."

Tuesday 10th October

8:18am

Jail sentence served so far: 4 days, 15 hours, 55 minutes and 20 seconds.

That stupid wolf should stick to cake decoration! I'm not giving up. Here's my new plan - it can't fail. I hope.

1. Have secret conversation with Rumplestiltskin (he's being freed from prison tomorrow).

2. Make him hide Bethany in the tallest tower in the land, with a fierce dragon guarding the door so she can't escape.

3. Make sure no one suspects me.

4. Get out of here somehow.

5. Marry the prince.

6. Be a rich princess. Live happily ever after. Heh heh heh heh heh!

Cinderella:	Hey Rumpy. I hear you're being freed from this place soon. I've got a job for you.
Rumplestiltskin:	What's it worth?
Cinderella:	A bag of gold.
Rumplestiltskin:	Don't be silly. You haven't got a bag of gold.
Cinderella:	I will have if you do this job. I'll be rich!

Rumplestiltskin: What do you want me to do?

Cinderella: Take my stepsister, Bethany Big Nose, and hide her in the highest tower in the land.

Rumplestiltskin: What? Princess Bethany?

Cinderella: That's right. And put a dragon at the bottom of the tower to make sure she can't escape. Then I'll break out of here, take her place and be the princess.

Rumplestiltskin: Oh, you *will* be rich! In that case it'll cost you two bags of gold.

Cinderella: It's a deal. Just don't let anyone find out it was me that sent you.

Rumplestiltskin: My lips are sealed.

Cinderella: And don't get her to guess your name.

Rumplestiltskin: But I always give them three guesses!

Cinderella: Yes – and you always get caught!

Wednesday 11th October
Time in this awful jail so far: 5 days, 5 hours, 5 minutes and 5 seconds.

Haven't heard how Rumplestiltskin got on. Hope he hasn't made a mess of it. Planning to take my mind off it for a bit by listening to the radio - there's a new one in the prison common room. I think *The Beauty and the Beast Show* is on tonight - my favourite!

Beauty: A huge welcome to all our listeners. I'm Beauty and you're listening to *The Beauty and the Beast Show* on Radio Fairytale. It's not often we have a royal visitor on the show, but today I'm delighted to welcome our very own Princess Bethany. How are you this evening, Your Royal Highness, after your narrow escape this morning?

Bethany: I'm OK, thank you.

Beast: But you were confronted by a desperate villain, Ma'am!

Bethany: I don't know why everyone is making such a fuss, Beast. It was just a little old man who said he was going to lock me in the tallest tower in the land.

Beauty: That sounds terrifying!

Bethany: Not at all. I told him I didn't want to be locked in the tallest tower and he said, "I'm not supposed to tell you this but I'll let you off if you can guess my name. I'll give you three guesses."

Beast: What happened then?

Bethany: I told him I knew he was Rumplestiltskin. Everyone who reads the *Daily Sparkle* knows it. His face was all over the front page last year when he was arrested for trying to snatch that queen's baby.

Beauty: That's not the end of the story, though, is it?

Bethany: No, the poor man seemed very cross that I knew his name and he stamped so hard that he fell through the floor. Well, several floors in fact! He ended up in the dungeon with a broken leg. He's in hospital now. I hope he gets better soon.

Beast: Thank you very much for letting us know what happened, Princess Bethany. Next up, we have St George to help us with our dragon makeover ...

STILL Wednesday

That stupid Rumplestiltskin failed! Can you believe it? I'm fed up with working with idiots!

I'll show *him*!

Dear Rumplestiltskin,

~~Sorry to hear that my dear friend~~
~~Nearly met a sticky end.~~
~~This card is sent from me to you,~~
~~With get well wishes sweet and true.~~

You really should have listened to me –
I said DON'T give her guesses three!
Now you're in a sorry plight,
And I have to say, it serves you right!

Cinders

Onceuponatime Town Prison
Gingerbread House Lane
Onceuponatime Town
12th October

Dear Mumsie,

I'm sorry for stealing your tarts and taking them clean away, after you'd worked so hard on that lovely summer day. Please remember that I did bring them back – well, the one I hadn't scoffed – and that I vow never to steal again.

It's not too bad in prison. There's a strange girl called Cinderella in my basket weaving class. She looks very angry and mutters to herself all the time. Yesterday I heard her say, "Stupid Rumplestiltskin, stupid wolf ... do it myself ... need a spell ... will have to go back to godmother." She's most odd.

Hope you and Daddy are well.
Love,
Your son, the Knave of Hearts xx

Dear Fairy Godmother,

I thought you'd like these songs. Read the play list carefully. These songs really convey a message, if you catch my drift!

Cinders x

Get Me Out Of Here Playlist

Help
The Dung Beetles

You can do magic
Tinkerbell and the Lost Boys

Set me free
Genie of the lamp

I want to break free
Rapunzel

Please, please help me
Dung Beetles remix

Don't let me down
Foxy and the Gingerbread Man

Do as I say
Old King Cole and The Fiddlers Three

You'll be sorry if you don't
The Snow Queen

Godmother Gossip Online
Keep up with the latest Fairy Tales!

The prestigious Godmother of the Year Award is coming up soon. So who's going to win that sparkly golden wand this time? Eat your hearts out, fairy godmothers everywhere – it's me! And here's what I've done to deserve it.

I have magicked my client, Cinderella Nottapenny, out of prison and turned her into a Princess Bethany look-alike. Even her own father wouldn't be able to tell the difference. And why, I hear you ask? Simple. Because she wants to live every girl's dream and be the princess. Think of the fun I'll have with my golden wand when I'm official F. G. to the future Queen! Watch this space.

p.s. I've bewitched this blog so the Palace Guard can't read it.

Fairytale Hospital Discharge Form

Please fill in, explaining why you are leaving hospital against the doctor's advice.

Patient's name
I'll give you three guesses.

Consultant
Dr Foster from Gloucester

Medical problem
Broken leg

Reason for leaving hospital
I want my two bags of gold so I'm hobbling off to the palace again to kidnap Princess Bethany. Oops! I'm not supposed to tell you that.

Signed
Rumplestiltskin. Oops! I'm not supposed to tell you that either.

Whiskers: Hey Scratch, come down to the kitchen! I've found some delicious chocolate cheesecake in the fridge. I'm so glad we moved to the palace when Bethany married the prince. It's great!

Scratch: Why don't you come up to the banquet hall instead? There are loads of yummy crumbs under the table here!

Whiskers: But this is cheesecake! Chocolate cheesecake! Ah, here comes Princess Bethany.

Scratch: You're seeing things. Princess Bethany is here in the banquet hall, tucking into some muffins. There are good pickings under her chair.

Whiskers: No, she's down here. I'm waving to her. Whoa! That's odd. She tried to whack me with a cucumber.

Scratch: That's not Princess Bethany then. She'd never do such a nasty thing!

Whiskers: You're right – it's that awful Cinderella! I'd know her smell anywhere. She must be disguised as Princess Bethany. Why would she do that? Oh, watch out Scratch, she's heading up the stairs!

Scratch: She's here now. Wow! She does look like Princess Bethany! Oh no – she's grabbed the real Bethany and locked her in a cupboard!

Whiskers: We've got to help Bethany! I'm scampering up the stairs to help.

Scratch: A man with crutches has just come hobbling into the room. Hang on, I know him – it's that silly man who's always asking people to guess his name.

Whiskers: That'll be Rumplestiltskin. Keep out of his way. He's a baddie!

Scratch: He's not that bad. He's just rugby-tackled Cinders to the floor! Listen!

Rumplestiltskin [in background]: It's no good trying to guess my name 'cos I've learned my lesson and my lips are sealed!

Cinderella [also in background]: Let go of me, you idiot! And I don't need to guess your name. It's Rumplestiltskin.

[A loud **CRASH** interrupts the phone call]

Whiskers: What was that noise?

Scratch: That was Rumplestiltskin. I think he was cross. He stamped his foot and fell through the floor, right down to the dungeons, I reckon! Oh no, Cinders is free again. I'm off to bite her ankles!

Whiskers: I'm almost there. I'll figure out a way to free Princess Bethany.

PRINCESS SAVED IN RODENT RESCUE

Ding dong bell, Cinders back in cell

says royal reporter Tommy Stout

ONCEUPONATIME TOWN WAS stunned yesterday by the news that convict Cinderella Nottapenny had been up to her old tricks.

She broke out of prison (thanks to a certain fairy godmother, who has now been arrested). Then, disguised as Princess Bethany, Cinderella entered the palace, where she attacked her royal stepsister before shoving her into a cupboard.

Her evil plan to take Princess Bethany's place was thwarted by two off-duty detective mice, who bravely stopped Cinders in her tracks long enough for the palace guards to arrest her and take her back to prison. Then the mice released poor Princess Bethany.

"I was sitting in the dark, unsure what was going on, when I heard gnawing at the lock," said the princess, "and the next moment I was free."

The newly-knighted Sir Whiskers and Sir Scratch have been granted a lifetime supply of chocolate cheesecake by Prince Charming as a thank you for rescuing his young wife.

"We'll all live happily ever after now," said the happy prince.

Added note: We apologise for the quality of the photo as our official photographer, Mr Dumpty, fell off a chair. He is now back in his usual hospital bed.